TIME SPIES

Where will they go next?

**The postcard predicts
an athletic adventure!**

TimeSpies

TIME SPIES
Horses in the Wind

By Candice Ransom
Illustrated by Greg Call

MIRRORSTONE

HORSES IN THE WIND

©2007 Wizards of the Coast, Inc.

Published by Wizards of the Coast, Inc. TIME SPIES, MIRRORSTONE and their respective logos are trademarks of Wizards of the Coast, Inc., in the U.S.A. and other countries.

Printed in the U.S.A.

Cover and Interior art by Greg Call
First Printing: November 2007

9 8 7 6 5 4 3 2 1

ISBN: 978-0-7869-4355-5
620-10989740-001-EN

Library of Congress Cataloging-in-Publication Data

Ransom, Candice F., 1952-
  Horses in the wind / Candice Ransom ; illustrated by Greg Call.
    p. cm. — (Time spies ; [7])
  "Mirrorstone."
  Summary: When the magical spyglass transports the three Chapman children to 1938 Maryland, they attend the race between two champion racehorses—War Admiral, the high-spirited favorite, and Seabiscuit, the western underdog.
  ISBN 978-0-7869-4355-5
  [1. Time travel—Fiction. 2. Horse racing—Fiction. 3. Seabiscuit (Race horse)—Fiction. 4. War Admiral (Race horse)—Fiction. 5. Magic—Fiction. 6. Brothers and sisters—Fiction.] I. Call, Greg, ill. II. Title.
  PZ7.R1743Hor 2007
  [Fic]—dc22

                                                                    2007017888

U.S., CANADA,
ASIA, PACIFIC, & LATIN AMERICA
Wizards of the Coast, Inc.
P.O. Box 707
Renton, WA 98057-0707
+1-800-324-6496

EUROPEAN HEADQUARTERS
Hasbro UK Ltd
Caswell Way
Newport, Gwent NP9 0YH
GREAT BRITAIN
Please keep this address for your records

Visit our Web site at www.mirrorstonebooks.com

To Ashley,
who has always loved horses

Contents

The Sports Star

Alex Chapman aimed and kicked his soccer ball.

"Over the birdbath!" he cried, predicting the ball's path. "Goal!"

Instead the soccer ball rolled slowly across the backyard and stopped several feet before the base of the birdbath.

Alex plopped down on the back porch step beside his older sister.

"I can't kick anymore," he said.

Mattie pushed her hair behind one ear. "You're just out of practice."

Alex frowned. "I played sports all the time back in Maryland. There's no one here to play with."

"I miss my friends back in Maryland too," Mattie said. "No offense, but I never see anybody but you and Sophie."

"Gee, thanks." He made a face.

"You know what I mean," Mattie said. "I like it here in Virginia. And this summer has been great, but . . ."

"Yeah," agreed Alex.

It *had* been an exciting summer. Alex never dreamed that the old house his parents had bought and turned into a bed and breakfast would hide a cool secret!

First, he, Mattie, and Sophie had discovered the hidden door leading into the mysterious third-floor tower room. Then they found the magic spyglass that sent them on thrilling adventures. They had met George Washington, been in Harry Houdini's magic show, and even climbed a giant beanstalk into the sky.

"I wish some kids lived around here," he said. "Boys my age. We could play soccer. Or football. Or both!"

"Just what I'd love, more eight-year-old boys," said Mattie. "Why can't a nine-year-old *girl* move next door?"

"For one thing, there *is* no next door. Our house is the only one for miles." Alex slumped, his chin on his fists.

Just then Sophie skipped around the corner of the house. She carried her stuffed elephant, Ellsworth, in one hand and a limp bunch of daisies in the other.

"Sophie doesn't miss anything back in Maryland," Alex said.

"That's because she's five," said Mattie. "Stuff is easier when you're a little kid."

"Alex!" Sophie cried when she saw him. "Play horses with me?"

"Aw, Soph," he groaned. "We played horses last night. And the night before."

"Ple-e-ease?"

"All right." With a deep sigh, Alex got up and walked out into the yard.

Sophie pointed at him. "You be the white horse with the black mane and tail. And I'll be the black horse with the white mane and tail."

"Why can't I be the black horse for a change?" he asked. "I'm always the white horse."

"Because I said so." She galloped across the yard, whinnying.

Alex galloped too, but he refused to make "horsey" noises. Sophie's game was so dumb.

There were no rules. All they did was run around.

"Can we quit now?" Alex asked. He was tired already.

"No!" Sophie reared, pretending to paw the air.

The back door opened and his father came out. Alex galloped to the porch, hoping Sophie wouldn't notice.

"We have a guest coming any minute," Mr. Chapman told Alex and Mattie. "I'm working out back and may not hear the car. Your mother is busy getting the Jefferson Suite ready."

Alex shot a look at Mattie. The Jefferson Suite! That meant one thing—the arrival of a new Travel Guide!

Guests who stayed in the third-floor Jefferson Suite had special powers. They helped send the kids back in time on different missions.

Their parents didn't know this, of course. Alex could imagine what his mother and father would say if he told them about their secret adventures.

"Who's the new guest?" Mattie asked Mr. Chapman.

"I only know the person is an Olympic medalist," he replied.

"Wow!" Alex exclaimed. "What sport?"

"I have no idea. Your mother is fixing the room now. Let us know if the guest arrives." Mr. Chapman went back indoors.

"An Olympic champion," Mattie said, awestruck. "We've never had anybody that famous stay here before."

"I bet he's a big soccer star," said Alex.

"Or a gymnast."

Sophie galloped up. "You quit the game!" she said to Alex.

"Sorry, Soph, but a new Travel Guide is on

his way. You'd rather go back in time than play horses, wouldn't you?"

She frowned. "No. And it's a her."

"Her what?"

Just then Alex heard the crunch of tires on gravel.

"He's here!" Alex jumped off the porch. Mattie and Sophie followed him around to the front of the house.

A young woman with long brown hair stepped out of a red car.

"Are you the Olympic star?" Alex asked, running up. "Where's your medal?" He expected to see the medal around her neck.

She laughed. "The medal is kind of heavy to wear."

"What kind of a medal is it?" Mattie asked.

"A silver from the 1996 Olympic Games in Atlanta," the woman replied.

"Women's soccer?" Alex asked hopefully. The women's soccer team back then had been awesome.

She shook her head. "Riding."

He was puzzled. "Riding . . . like, a bobsled?"

"A horse."

"Horse!" Sophie shrieked. "I'm a black horse with a white mane and tail!" She whinnied as proof.

Alex said quickly, "That's really our sister, Sophie. I'm Alex and this is Mattie. I'll take your bag."

"Thank you. I'm Carol Hawley." She walked up to the house as Sophie trotted beside her. "I used to play horses when I was your age."

"I'm not playing," Sophie said. "I really *am* a horse."

Embarrassed, Alex opened the front door and called, "Mom!"

Mrs. Chapman hurried into the hall. "Welcome to Gray Horse Inn."

"Mom makes great shortbread," Mattie told the guest, "and lemonade."

"Sounds wonderful," Ms. Hawley said. "I've been visiting Thoroughbred farms all day. Lemonade and shortbread would hit the spot."

"The kids will show you into the Keeping Room," said Mrs. Chapman. She went into the kitchen.

"What kind of farms were you at today?" Mattie asked, leading the way into the big room with sofas, chairs, and a fireplace.

"Thoroughbred horses," Ms. Hawley replied. "I train horses and teach riding. One of my clients wants a new horse. I found one and bought it for her."

Mrs. Chapman came in with a tray.

"Mom, this lady bought a horse!" Sophie

exclaimed. "A thurby!"

"T*horoughbred*!" Alex said. All this horse talk was boring. "I'm going back outside. I need to practice kicking."

Mattie glared at him as he passed her chair. He knew why. They always chatted with the new Travel Guide to find out more about their upcoming adventure.

What kind of adventure would a horse rider send them on? Why couldn't the Olympic star have been a soccer player or a football player? A *real* sport.

Ka-thump! *Ka-thump*!

Alex sat up in bed. W*hat* was that noise? He threw the covers back and shuffled over to open his door. Sophie galloped down the hall, heading for the stairs. D*oesn't she walk anywhere anymore*? he wondered.

"Come on!" she said, whipping around.

10

"Time for breakfast. Aren't you excited to go on a new adventure?"

No, he wasn't. It would probably be all about a bunch of dumb old *thurbys*.

Sighing, he got dressed and went downstairs to the dining room.

Mattie and Sophie were already sitting with Carol Hawley. Sophie gazed raptly at the new Travel Guide. She wasn't even paying attention to Ellsworth.

Alex poked Sophie as he slid into the chair next to her. "Quit staring!" he whispered.

"Ms. Hawley was telling us about the Olympics," Mattie said to Alex. "She was in the three-day event. Jumping, a cross-country course, and that horse ballet thing."

"Dressage," said Ms. Hawley. "It's harder than jumping."

"She has six *Thoroughbreds*," Sophie announced.

"What's so special about those horses?" Mattie asked.

"They are the fastest, most valuable breed," Ms. Hawley replied. "Did you know that the first American Thoroughbred horse came from England to Virginia? The horse was named Bulle Rock. Virginia became famous for its horses and many horse farms."

Alex shoveled eggs and sausage in his mouth. "Horses are all alike."

"Not really," said Ms. Hawley. "Thoroughbreds are good jumpers and show horses. But they are really bred for racing. Back in Colonial times, lots of towns had a 'Race Street.' People would watch horse races in the middle of town."

"I'd rather watch car racing." Gripping the edge of his plates with both hands, he pretended to steer. "*Vroom, vroom!*"

Mattie shot him a look that said, *Quit it*.

Ms. Hawley pointed to a picture of Monticello hanging on the wall. "I went to Thomas Jefferson's home yesterday. Did you know Jefferson used to watch horse races when he was a student at the college of William and Mary in Williamsburg? He was also an excellent rider."

Alex yawned behind a piece of toast. He had ridden horses, sort of, on several adventures back in time. It wasn't such a big deal.

Ms. Hawley glanced at her watch. "Uh-oh. I need to be at Evening Star Farms in an hour. I'm signing the papers for the new horse. But first I want to send a postcard—"

Mattie leaped up and handed her a postcard from the stack on the sideboard.

"A lot of horse people travel this way," Ms. Hawley said, scribbling on the back of the card. "They'll want to know about the Gray Horse Inn. If I write to one friend, he'll spread the word."

She dropped the postcard in a tray on the sideboard, and then hurried out of the dining room.

Mattie pounced on the card. "Whoa!"

"What?" Alex got up to look.

As always, the picture on the postcard had changed. Instead of the photograph of the Gray Horse Inn, there was a picture of stadium packed with people.

Alex felt a quiver of excitement. "That looks like a football stadium!"

Mattie frowned. "I hope we're not going to a football game back in time."

"I hope we do! What's the message say?"

Mattie flipped the card over.

He'll win by five.

"We *are* going back to a big game. And the team will win by five points. Woo-hoo! Let's go!"

Alex dashed out of the dining room and up the stairs. Mattie and Sophie ran after him.

On the third floor Alex swiveled the small bookcase, revealing a low passage into the tower room. He scrambled through and sprinted over to the desk, the only piece of furniture in the room.

Sophie crawled through, clutching Ellsworth. Mattie followed, closing the book-case-panel behind her.

"How come you're in such a rush all of a sudden?" she asked. "You were barely nice to the Travel Guide. I didn't think you were even interested in this mission."

"I want to get to the game!" He retrieved a wooden box from the desk.

Inside, nestled in velvet, was a brass spyglass. Alex held the spyglass by one end. "Ready?"

"Ready." Sophie clasped the middle of the spyglass, holding Ellsworth in her other hand.

Mattie grasped the other end.

Instantly, Alex felt the familiar tingling beneath his fingers. Strange symbols appeared on the brass cylinder. The magic was working! He closed his eyes. Red and white and green sparks whirled behind his eyelids. The floor seemed to drop away.

Then ... *thump!*

His feet hit something solid. Before opening his eyes, Alex drew in a deep breath. He smelled the rich, fresh scent of dirt and grass.

Yes! he thought. He was on a playing field.

2

Horse Spies

Alex opened his eyes. He was standing on grass, but it wasn't a football field. A crowd of people pushed him up against a waist-high wooden rail. Men, teenage boys, and a few women stared at a dirt oval track just beyond the rail.

Alex glanced around for Mattie and Sophie. *Did they get lost in this mob*? he thought

Then he saw Mattie squeeze between two men, towing Sophie.

"We're here," she said.

"Where's here?" Alex asked.

Mattie pointed to a newspaper tucked under a man's arm. "He's carrying a copy of *The Baltimore Sun*," she said excitedly. "We must be back in Maryland!" She squinted to read the date. "October 30, 1938."

"But *where* are we?" Alex wanted to know. "What is this place?"

A murmur rippled through the crowd. Everyone looked in the same direction. Alex looked too.

Thoppity, thoppity, thop!

A sleek black horse breezed down the track. A man not much bigger than Mattie crouched over the horse's neck. The horse passed by so fast, it was a black blur.

The boy next to Alex pushed a button on a stopwatch. "Two minutes, four seconds," the boy said.

"Is that good?" Alex asked. The boy seemed to be Mattie's age.

"Good!" The boy stared at him. "What else do you expect from the fastest horse in the East!"

The black horse pranced back up the track. Sunshine glinted off its gleaming coat. Suddenly the horse reared, pawing the air. Its rider pulled the reins back. When the horse calmed down, the rider rode him off the track.

Another horse walked onto the track, ridden by another small man. This horse was brown and fatter than the black horse. He was followed by a golden horse.

"I bet that's a palomino," Mattie said.

The golden horse's rider slid off and held up a small wooden box. He pushed a button and the box made a clanging sound, like an old-fashioned alarm clock.

The brown horse took off down the track. The boy next to Alex checked his stopwatch.

"Two minutes, fifty-two seconds," he muttered. "He'll have to do better."

The brown horse trotted back to the starting line. The bell clanged again and the horse zipped down the track. He ran several times before his rider led him off the track, along with the man on the golden horse.

The crowd broke up, streaming through a gate in the rail.

"Come on," Alex told Mattie and Sophie. "Let's follow the boy with the watch."

He kept an eye on the teenage boy as people headed toward several brightly painted buildings. Most filed down a right-hand path, but the kids stayed with the boy, who chose a path to the left. At the end of the path was a long, low building.

Alex stopped just behind a signpost. He

and Mattie and Sophie could see what was going on but not be noticed.

The boy pushed through a knot of people gathered at the tall double doors and stepped inside. Alex recognized the bell-ringing man standing by the doors, as if on guard.

"Mr. Smith, will Seabiscuit beat War Admiral?" a man with a notebook asked. Alex figured he must be a reporter.

A second man waved his pen. "What are Seabiscuit's chances, Mr. Smith? He seemed a little sluggish today."

Mr. Smith crossed his arms. He didn't reply.

The first man stuffed his notebook in his coat pocket. "C'mon, fellas. We won't get a story here. At least they'll talk to us in War Admiral's barn."

The reporters walked away, grumbling.

Mr. Smith opened one of the big barn

doors. The boy came out, holding the brown horse's bridle.

"They've gone for now," Mr. Smith told him. "Cool him down good."

"Yessir."

Clucking his tongue, the boy led the horse around to the side. In the middle stood a device with arms that reminded Alex of a merry-go-round. The boy hooked the horse to one of the arms and began leading the horse around in a circle.

"Let's go talk to him," Alex said to the others. "Maybe he'll give us a clue what our mission is."

The kids approached the boy, who frowned at them.

"You were at the track," he said to Alex. "What are you doing here? Are you spies for War Admiral's barn?"

Alex blinked. They were spies, sort of, but

not for a barn. "We just came over to say hi. I'm Alex and these are my sisters, Mattie and Sophie."

"Can I pet the horse?" Sophie asked. She was so excited, she didn't even introduce Ellsworth, Alex noticed.

"When he's cooled off," the boy said. "I'm Bobby, Seabiscuit's hot walker."

"What kind of a job is that?" Mattie asked.

"After racehorses work out, they need to walk to cool down," Bobby replied. "It's bad for their muscles if they don't."

Alex waved his hand toward the track. "Do they have car races here?"

Bobby laughed. "Car races! You're at the Pimlico racetrack. It's for horses!" He looked at them. "You don't know, do you?"

"Know what?" asked Mattie.

"About the race." Bobby gawked at them.

"If you haven't heard about the match race between War Admiral and Seabiscuit, how come you're here?"

Alex exchanged a look with Mattie. Whenever they went back in time, there was always a sticky moment like this one.

"Uh—we just dropped in," he said.

Bobby shook his head. "You kids must be from Mars. Seabiscuit and War Admiral are the two most famous horses in America. They are finally going to race each other the day after tomorrow. Then we'll find out which horse is the best."

"Seabiscuit is," said Sophie.

"You bet he is," Bobby said. "But War Admiral is a Triple Crown winner. He won the Kentucky Derby, the Preakness, and the Belmont. Not many horses have won all three races. And he's the son of Man O'War."

"Who's that?" asked Alex.

"Man O'War was the greatest horse ever," Bobby replied. "War Admiral has his father's speed."

"If War Admiral is so fast, what's the big deal about Seabiscuit?" Mattie asked.

"People admire War Admiral," said Bobby. "But Seabiscuit is the horse everybody loves. Years ago, nobody wanted him. He had bad legs. They didn't believe he could win races. But ol' Biscuit proved them wrong."

"What happened?" Alex wanted to know. "I mean, how did he get to be famous?"

"Charles Howard bought Seabiscuit," Bobby replied. "And then Mr. Smith, his trainer, helped Seabiscuit get better. Soon the Biscuit was winning races."

"If the race is the day after tomorrow," Alex asked, "what are all these people doing here now?"

Bobby unhooked Seabiscuit from the

merry-go-round device. "Reporters, mostly. Like I said, this is the biggest story since Roosevelt became president. A lot of people want Seabiscuit to win. But just as many are rooting for War Admiral. All the reporters are looking for a big scoop."

"Why don't they just wait until the race is over?" asked Mattie.

Bobby led Seabiscuit back to the building. "The reporters write stories for their newspapers or radio stations every day. Folks are eager for news about the horses."

Seabiscuit dipped his head toward a large metal chest just outside.

"No," Bobby told him, tugging on the bridle. "It's not time to eat." To the kids, he added, "Seabiscuit can't pass a feed bin without stopping."

They went inside. Two rows of horse stalls faced a long wooden aisle. Bins for hay and oats lined the aisle. Bridles, halters, and brushes hung on the walls.

Bobby walked Seabiscuit to a large stall. A German shepherd lying by a feed bucket jumped up and began barking. Alex and Mattie backed away, but Sophie smiled at the huge dog.

"It's okay, Silver," Bobby said and the dog stopped barking. "Silver is Seabiscuit's guard dog."

Alex couldn't believe any horse was so important that he needed his own guard dog. He thought of something. "A minute ago you called us spies. What did you mean by that?"

"Some people want to know how Mr. Smith plans to beat War Admiral," Bobby said.

"What do you mean?" Alex asked. "Won't the horses just run around the track until one of them wins?"

"It's not that simple, kid," Bobby replied. "Every race is different. The tracks are different. Mr. Smith works Seabiscuit over this track every day to see how fast he goes. He thinks about the difference between the horses. War Admiral is bigger and runs like the wind."

Bobby swung open the stall door. Seabiscuit walked in. The golden horse was already in the stall, munching on some hay.

"That's Pumpkin," Bobby said. "He's Seabiscuit's barn buddy. So is this little guy. Hey, Pocatell."

A small spotted dog scampered into the stall.

Alex watched Bobby throw a soft plaid blanket over Seabiscuit, and then remove the horse's halter and bridle.

"You can pet him now," Bobby said to Sophie.

Eagerly she reached up and stroked the horse's nose. "He nibbled my hand!" she giggled.

"He wants a treat." Bobby took a carrot from a mesh bag.

"You really like this horse, don't you?" said Alex.

Bobby nodded. "Thanks to Seabiscuit, I have a job. Horse racing is my life. And it's Seabiscuit's. All we both needed was a chance.

Because Seabiscuit is small and not as flashy as other horses, people ignored him."

"Did they ignore you too?" asked Mattie.

"They used to. But Mr. Smith says I'll be a great jockey in a few years."

Alex frowned. "What are you—twelve? Can you be a horse rider that young?"

Bobby laughed so hard he dropped the bag of carrots. "Twelve! Wait'll I tell the Iceman and Mr. Smith!" He wiped his eyes. "I'm *twenty*."

"Twenty!" Alex blurted. "But you're—"

"Little?" Bobby grinned. "Jockeys have to be small. Horses can't run fast carrying a big, heavy rider."

Alex flushed. "Sorry. You must think we're really dumb."

"It's okay. You've just proved you can't be spies from War Admiral's barn."

"We're not spies for War Admiral," said

Mattie. "We want Seabiscuit to win."

Sophie looked up from feeding the horse. "He will."

"That's the spirit," said Bobby. "I'm sorry for being so suspicious. It's just I have to be careful. I can't let anybody find out about Seabiscuit's training secrets."

Alex nodded. Suddenly he knew their mission. They had been sent back in time to help Seabiscuit win the big race.

Instead of being Time Spies, they were now horse spies.

3

The Big-Eared Man

"I have to feed Grog," said Bobby. He left Seabiscuit's stall and unlatched the door of the next stall.

The kids followed him.

"Wow!" said Alex when he saw the horse inside. "That horse looks just like Seabiscuit!"

"You think so?" Bobby whistled an aimless tune as he scooped oats into Grog's feed trough. "My chores are over for a while. You'll have to leave."

"Can we come back and visit Seabiscuit?" Sophie asked.

"You bet. See you kids later."

Outside, Alex said, "I figured out our mission. We're here to help Seabiscuit."

Mattie nodded. "We definitely want him to win. He's so sweet."

"We have to keep War Admiral's spies away from here," said Alex. He looked at the people milling around. Any one of them could be a spy. "Where do we start?"

"Let's go to War Admiral's place," Mattie suggested. "If we see a guy there and then see him here, he could be a spy."

"Good idea. I think the other horse's barn is this way," Alex said, striding down the second path. Mattie and Sophie hurried after him.

At War Admiral's barn, the kids stopped in amazement. At least a hundred reporters and photographers clustered around the closed doors.

"Seems like War Admiral is more popular than Seabiscuit," Alex said.

Just then one of the double doors slid open and a man in a checked shirt came out. The nose of a black horse could be seen poking over the stall door just inside.

Immediately, photographers raised their cameras. Flashbulbs burst. Reporters surged forward, pencils poised over their notebooks.

"Mr. Conway!" several voices clamored.

"How is War Admiral today?" others called. "Is he sleeping well in Man O'War's old stall?"

The man in the checked shirt waved his arms angrily. "Go away! Leave my horse alone!"

"Who's that guy?" Alex asked a gum-chewing photographer next to him.

"That's Mr. George Conway," the man replied. "He's War Admiral's trainer."

"He's kind of grouchy," said Mattie.

The photographer laughed. "Everybody connected with this race is keyed up. Fans have wanted a match race between War Admiral and Seabiscuit for so long. Now it's almost here and we're all on edge."

"What did that guy mean about Man O'War's stall?" Alex asked.

"War Admiral is staying in the same stall as Man O'War," said the photographer. "Man O'War was his father. Man O'War won the Preakness race here at Pimlico back in 1920."

Alex looked at the sleek black head over the stall door. "So War Admiral is a star."

"Just like Babe Ruth." The photographer cracked his gum.

Mr. Conway stamped back inside the barn, slamming the door after him. Several reporters and photographers drifted away, but most stayed.

"We can't find out anything here," Mattie said. "Let's go back to Seabiscuit's barn." She turned without looking and accidentally bumped into a man.

"Watch where you're going!" the man snapped. He glared at Mattie before stomping away.

Alex noticed the grumpy man had ears that stuck out like car doors.

"Why is everybody so touchy?" asked Mattie. "It's just a horse race!"

"It's no ordinary race," Alex said. "This is the biggest thing to happen in America in 1938 and we never heard about it! We don't even know which horse won."

"I do," said Sophie. "Seabiscuit."

"How do you know?" Mattie asked her.

"I just do," Sophie said.

Alex sighed. Sophie was sometimes right, but they couldn't go by the feelings of a five-year-old. They still had a mission to accomplish.

"It's getting late," he said. "We'd better get back to Seabiscuit's barn."

Bobby was standing by the side of the building, gazing at the clouds masking the setting sun. "I hope it doesn't rain anymore," he said. "The track needs to dry out."

Chairs surrounded a small table. A string-tied packet of sandwiches and two cans of pork and beans lay on the table.

"Hungry? I bought more than I can eat." Bobby opened the cans and stuck spoons in them.

"Thanks," said Mattie.

Alex sat in one of the chairs and took a sandwich from the pile. "You sure you don't mind us eating your food?"

"I got used to sharing when I was riding the rails." At Alex's puzzled look, Bobby explained, "Hopping trains. That's how I got around until Mr. Smith hired me. Me and a lot of other guys slept in boxcars or in shacks in railroad yards."

"Why didn't you go home?" asked Sophie.

"My dad had a little grocery store. I worked in it. But then the banks ran out of money and Dad lost the store."

"How can banks run out of money?" asked Alex. "That's what banks are *for.*"

"We're in the Great Depression, aren't we?" said Mattie. "I read about that in school—I mean, I've *heard* about it."

"We're in it all right." Bobby passed around the cans of beans. "Dad didn't need another mouth to feed so I left home. Traveled with men who didn't have jobs. I would still be out of work if it weren't for Mr. Smith. He hired me as a hot walker. He says I'll be an exercise boy pretty soon. And then I can train to be a jockey."

"Train?" said Alex. "Why? The horse does all the running."

Bobby laughed. "That's what you think! Did you know it's harder to be a jockey than a football quarterback? In a way, jockeys are stronger."

"No way!" Alex said.

"It's true. For one thing, jockeys don't just sit in the saddle. They lean over the horse's neck. Only the inside of their feet and their ankles touch the horse." He gripped the chair leg with the inside of one foot to demonstrate.

"How do the riders keep from falling off?" Mattie asked.

"It isn't easy," Bobby replied. "Horses are animals, not machines. Racehorses weigh about fourteen hundred pounds and run forty miles an hour. A jockey uses every muscle."

Alex still couldn't believe a horse rider was stronger than a quarterback.

Yawning, Bobby tossed the trash into a bin near the side door. "Time to hit the hay. Aren't you kids going home?"

"Well—uh," Alex began.

Bobby raised his hand. "Don't bother explaining. A lot of folks are down on their luck these days. I'm staying in the jockeys' quarters, but you can sleep in the next barn. It's empty."

"We will," said Mattie. "Thanks."

Bobby unlatched the door of the next barn. Two rows of stalls stretched to the end of the long building. "I'm going to check on Seabiscuit, then turn in."

"Can we come?" Sophie asked.

"Sure, but be quiet." Bobby led the way

41

back to Seabiscuit's barn. He stepped up on a cement stoop and opened a side door.

"How come we aren't going in the front door?" Alex asked.

"Mr. Smith is guarding it," Bobby replied. "Seabiscuit's groom is watching the back door. I'll lock this door when you go back outside."

Inside, the barn was dimly lit. Silver leaped to attention, but relaxed when he recognized Bobby. Pocatell snoozed in front of the stall door.

Pumpkin, the palomino, drowsed in the large stall, standing with his head down. Seabiscuit lay on his side in the deep straw, sound asleep.

"Biscuit is the only horse I've ever seen that lies down to sleep," said Bobby. "See you early tomorrow," he said to the horses.

"How early?" Alex wanted to know.

"Very early." Bobby lowered his voice to

a whisper. "That's one of Mr. Smith's secrets. He tries to train Seabiscuit at night or at dawn when other people aren't around. If it's not raining, that is. This morning it rained so we had to use the track after War Admiral's workout."

He opened the side door to let them out. "Good night."

Before they entered the empty barn, Alex stopped.

"Wait," he said. "Suppose someone from War Admiral's place is watching us? And he thinks the side door isn't being guarded?"

"You don't expect us to sleep outside, do you?" Mattie said. "It's cold!"

Alex spied the trash bin. Reaching in, he fished out the two bean cans and the string.

"What are you doing?" she asked. "There's no food left. Even *you* won't eat out of a garbage can."

"You'll see."

Alex put one of the chairs on the cement stoop in front of the side door. Kneeling, he tied one end of the string to the door handle. He wrapped the other end to the lid of one of the cans.

Carefully he pushed the lid into the opening of the second can and stacked them in the seat of the chair.

"What is *that*?" Mattie asked.

"An alarm," Alex explained. "If some-body tries to open the door, the cans will fall from the chair, make a noise, and we'll hear them."

She stared at him. "Where did you learn how to do that?"

He shrugged. "Maybe it's all the spy practice."

The kids went inside. Alex chose the stall closest to the door in case they heard some-thing. They fluffed straw to make beds.

Alex lay back in the straw. "Do you think Mr. Smith will take Seabiscuit out tonight or in the morning?"

"I don't know," came Mattie's sleepy voice.

Alex drifted off himself, dreaming about a black locomotive shaped like a horse barreling down the tracks.

Clatter! Crash!

Alex jumped up. "The alarm! It went off!" He tore out of the stall.

Mattie and Sophie ran after him, scattering straw. Alex jerked open the door.

In front of the turned-over chair, a man was rubbing his knee. When he saw the kids, he growled, "Who put this stuff here for me to trip over?"

"Sorry," Alex said innocently. "Aren't you out kind of late?"

"I was just checking to see if Seabiscuit is comfortable," the man replied. "Anyway, it's none of your business!"

The man limped down the path. In the streetlight, Alex could see the man's giant ears.

"Isn't he . . . ?" Mattie began.

Alex nodded. "Yeah, that's the guy you ran into at War Admiral's barn."

"I don't buy his story for a minute," said Mattie.

"Me neither." Alex watched the figure of the big-eared man grow smaller. "I wonder what he was *really* doing over here?"

"Maybe trying to hurt Seabiscuit?" Mattie said.

"No!" cried Sophie.

"Shh!" Alex said. "Nobody's going to touch Seabiscuit while we're around."

Secretly Alex wondered if they would be able to stop a big man like that from harming Seabiscuit . . . or them.

4

Touchdown!

"A-ch*ooo*!"

The sneeze woke Alex instantly. He sat up, flicking wisps of hay from his hair. "Who's there?"

"It's only me," Mattie said. "This hay is making me—" She sneezed again.

Alex glimpsed morning light out the window. He didn't even remember falling asleep.

"I hope we didn't miss Mr. Smith and

Seabiscuit," he said. He got up and peeked out the door.

Two huge shapes moved slowly in the morning mist. Alex recognized Pumpkin, with Mr. Smith on his back. Seabiscuit and his rider followed.

"Wake Sophie," Alex said. "They're going out right now! We need to make sure Big Ears doesn't spy on them."

By the time the kids reached the track, several people stood at the rail. A familiar face grinned at them.

"Here for the show?" Bobby asked them.

"I thought Mr. Smith trained Seabiscuit when nobody's around," said Alex.

"His plan doesn't always work. It's just an ordinary practice run, but people must think Seabiscuit will break track records."

Mr. Smith halted Pumpkin and slid off with his alarm bell. Before he turned around, people peppered him with questions.

"How's the Biscuit doing?" one man yelled.

"Did he sleep well?" another asked.

"Think he'll break as fast as War Admiral?"

Mr. Smith ignored the bystanders.

Seabiscuit's jockey looped the reins in one hand and walked him to the head of the track. He didn't look at any of the people along the rail or answer their questions either.

"Who's that guy riding Seabiscuit?" Alex asked.

"The Iceman?" Bobby answered. "His real name is George Woolf, but people call him the Iceman because he's so cool. Nothing bothers him when he's on a horse. But he's not Seabiscuit's regular jockey."

"Who is?" asked Mattie.

"Red Pollard. He's in the hospital." Bobby

shook his head sadly. "Red had a bad accident on a horse. The Iceman is riding Seabiscuit till Red recovers."

Alex stared at the jockey, who was adjusting the stirrups. He had never realized horse racing was such a dangerous sport.

Mr. Smith pushed the button on his bell.

Clang! Seabiscuit took off. He ran halfway down the track before George Woolf turned him back to the starting line. The trainer rang the bell and Seabiscuit flew off again.

"How come Seabiscuit doesn't run all the way around the track?" Alex asked.

"The Iceman is deliberately not running him too far or too fast," Bobby replied. "He doesn't want Seabiscuit to get tired."

"Why does Mr. Smith keep ringing the bell?" Mattie wanted to know.

"That's one of Mr. Smith's tricks," Bobby said. "War Admiral is a fast breaker. That means he takes off from the starting gate fast. Seabiscuit must learn to start fast too, or he may never catch up to War Admiral."

"I saw a horse race on the sports ch—" Alex stopped himself from saying "channel" in time. Television hadn't been invented yet. "Anyway, the horses jumped out of a boothlike thing."

Bobby nodded. "The starting gate. They aren't using a starting gate for this race. Seabiscuit and War Admiral will walk up to a line and the starter will ring a bell. That's why Mr. Smith is training Seabiscuit to run at the sound of a bell."

A man overhead Bobby. "Tom Smith can ring a school bell, but it won't make any difference. War Admiral will leave Seabiscuit in the dust."

"No, he won't!" Sophie said.

"War Admiral was named Horse of the Year last year," the man went on. "He won by four lengths at Belmont even after he had injured his foot!"

This horse talk was like another language. "What's a length?" Alex asked Bobby.

"The length of a horse. About eight feet. It's a way to measure distance," said Bobby. "War Admiral is a great horse, no doubt about it. But tomorrow we'll see the greatest horse of all."

After the workout, the horses and riders headed back to the barn. Alex, Mattie, and Sophie trailed after a group of reporters.

"Look!" Alex said. "It's Big Ears. I knew he'd be here!"

"He's talking to a guy with a camera," said Mattie. "I bet Big Ears is a reporter."

"That doesn't mean he can't be a spy too."

At the barn, more reporters and photographers jostled around the door. Seabiscuit and Pumpkin were nowhere in sight. Alex figured Mr. Smith had hustled the horses inside their stall.

"Can we get a shot of the Biscuit?" shouted the photographer with Big Ears.

Mr. Smith gave him a big smile. "You bet! Bring him out, Bobby!"

Bobby came out, leading the chestnut brown horse in his plaid blanket. Instantly, photographers' flashbulbs popped. Reporters busily jotted in their notebooks. The horse stood placidly, unconcerned by all the attention. Then Bobby took the horse back into the barn.

When he returned, he winked at the kids and said in a low voice, "That wasn't Seabiscuit. It was Grog! Mr. Smith wants Seabiscuit to rest. That's why he brought Grog along, to fool the reporters."

"Pretty smart," Alex said. "Seabiscuit has his own look-alike."

Then he felt eyes boring into his back. Glancing around, he saw Big Ears scowling at him. Alex wondered if the man's knee still hurt.

A teenage boy ran by. "Hey, Bobby! Football game in the infield. Exercise boys against the reporters. You coming?"

"I'll say!" Bobby turned to Alex. "Want to play?"

Alex felt a leap of excitement. "Yeah!"

He followed Bobby to the field inside the racetrack. The exercise boys were huddled at one end, while reporters and photographers were grouped at the other end.

"Sophie and I will sit over there," Mattie said, pointing to a grassy spot just outside the rail.

"We're playing six-man football," Bobby said to Alex.

"How do you play that way?" asked Alex.

"Every man is a receiver," Bobby said. "And you get more points for some plays. Okay, the first team to score twenty points wins."

After the teams were formed, Bobby and the other quarterback set the boundaries.

The teams lined up opposite each other with the ball on the ground between them. Then the quarterbacks flipped a coin to see which team would play offense. The exercise boys won the toss.

Rudy passed the ball to Bobby. Bobby dashed down the field to the end zone and scored a touchdown! The reporter's team grumbled after Bobby kicked the ball, earning the exercise boys a point after touchdown worth two points.

On the next play, Bobby was tackled. The ball sailed in the air. Alex ran back and forth, trying to find an opening.

Then he saw one of the other team members take off after Rudy, who had the ball. The guy was bigger than Alex, but Alex was faster. He tackled him from behind.

"Oof!" the man said as he hit the ground. "Get off me!"

"Uh-oh." Alex winced.

It was Big Ears. He glared at Alex as he scrambled to his feet.

"You!" Big Ears exclaimed. "What are you doing here? You're too young to be in the game."

Alex stood up straight. He wasn't going to let this guy scare him. "I'm not too young. Anyway, the others asked me to be on their team."

Big Ears pushed by him. "Stay out of my way, pipsqueak."

For the next several plays, the ball was carried by the reporters' team. But Bobby and

Rudy kept the other team from scoring any touchdowns. Then the exercise boys got possession of the ball and Bobby landed another touchdown. But the point after touchdown kick failed.

Alex yelled and cheered and ran until he was sweating. It felt so great to play a good game of football again.

He stopped to bend down and tie his sneaker. As he stood up, someone slammed into him. Then he noticed the person had the ball!

Without thinking, Alex snatched the ball away and ran toward the end zone as fast as Seabiscuit. His legs pumped as he passed the blurred faces of players on both teams. No one could catch him!

With a final burst of speed, Alex sprinted into his team's end zone. He bounced the ball on the ground and did a happy dance.

He had scored the winning touchdown!

Bobby and the other team members quickly surrounded him, slapping him on the back.

"You did it!" Bobby cried.

"Hooray for Alex!" someone yelled.

Alex felt himself being hoisted onto the shoulders of his teammates. They carried him down the infield, laughing and shouting.

When they set Alex down again, Rudy said to him, "You've got some nerve, kid. You grabbed the ball from Art Getsky."

"Who's he?"

"Only the most famous sports reporter for miles around. He's called Art 'Gets His Story' Getsky because he always gets his story. But today you got *him*!"

The exercise boys began leaving the field. Alex looked over at Mattie and Sophie and gave them a thumbs-up.

Someone shoved his shoulder. Alex twisted around, thinking it was another one of his teammates.

But it was Big Ears.

"You think you're a hotshot football player," he said to Alex. "Taking the ball away from me like that."

Alex gulped. Big Ears was "Gets His Story" Getsky?

Getsky shook his finger in Alex's face. "I know you've been following me, pip-squeak. War Admiral's owner promised me an exclusive story if War Admiral wins and I always get my story. Get my meaning? So stay out of my way or else!"

5

Sophie's Second Best Friend

"Where's everybody going?" Alex asked Bobby.

Bobby, the exercise boys, Mr. Smith, and George Woolf hustled down the path. Alex could tell they were going someplace important—their shoulders were stiff and they spoke to one another in tight, clipped voices.

"Track office," Bobby replied. "The officials are going to draw for the post position."

"What's that?" asked Mattie. She held Sophie's hand and hurried to keep up with the others.

"At the starting gate, the horses line up, from the rail to the outside edge of the track," Bobby explained. "The best position is right next to the rail. That's the shortest distance around the track."

"So it's good if Seabiscuit gets that spot," Alex said.

"Yeah, but it's the luck of the draw," Bobby said.

They reached a small building where other men were gathered. Alex recognized Mr. Conway, War Admiral's trainer. He also recognized Art Getsky.

The reporter saw him too. His eyes narrowed. "What are you three doing here? Kids aren't allowed in the track office."

Mr. Smith stepped between Alex and

Getsky. "Neither are reporters." He went inside the building.

"Let's wait over here," Alex said, pulling Mattie and Sophie away from the group of newsmen. He told them what Getsky had said after the game. "I think he plans to sabotage Seabiscuit's chances just so he can get an exclusive interview with War Admiral's owners."

"We'll have to keep an eye on him until the race tomorrow," Mattie said.

Just then the office door opened and the men filed out. Alex noticed that War Admiral's trainer was smiling. Mr. Smith was not.

The kids ran over to Bobby.

His face was downcast. "War Admiral drew the rail."

Art Getsky swooped down on them.

"Looks like it's all over for Seabiscuit," he said gleefully. "If he had gotten the rail, there was a *tiny* chance he would win. You might as well ship your horse back to California."

"Seabiscuit doesn't need the rail," Alex spoke up. "He'll beat that other horse no matter what."

Getsky ignored him, talking to Bobby. "You know Seabiscuit can't break away from the start like the Admiral. He just doesn't have the speed. Maybe he ought to pull a milk wagon." The reporter stalked off, laughing.

"That guy makes me so mad!" Alex clenched his fists.

"That's what this race is doing to people," Bobby said, shaking his head. "They are practically getting in fights over which horse will win."

The kids walked back to the barn with Bobby. Alex glanced over his shoulder several times to make sure Getsky wasn't trailing them.

In front of the barn, Mr. Smith paced in a circle. "I just went over to the racetrack," he said to Bobby. "The tractor is working, but the ground is still wet from all the rain. Will anything go right for this race?"

He went inside the barn.

"What's he talking about?" Mattie asked Bobby. "I didn't see any tractor on the racetrack."

"You've only been at the practice track," Bobby replied. "On the real track, by the grandstand, tractors harrow the dirt to help dry it."

"Can't horses run on mud?" Alex asked.

"Not very well." He blew out a puff of air. "If the track doesn't dry out by tomorrow afternoon, there might not even *be* a race!"

Alex shifted from one foot to the other. He had been standing by the side door for about an hour. Guard duty, he decided, was boring.

Bobby had once again shared his supper with them, and then left for the evening. The kids split up to watch the doors of Seabiscuit's barn—Mattie at the back door, Alex at the side door, and Sophie at the front door.

If any of them spied Art Getsky, they were supposed to whistle and the others would come.

Alex felt nervous about leaving Sophie to watch the front door. She was small enough to hide behind the feed bin, but she might fall asleep or something.

He left his post and walked around the side of the barn. No one was in sight, including Sophie.

Maybe she got lonely and went to talk to Mattie, he thought and headed in that direction.

But at the back of the barn, he only saw Mattie slumped against the wall.

"Where's Sophie?" he asked.

Mattie stared at him. "What do you mean? Isn't she out front?"

He shook his head. "I just checked. She's not there."

"We've got to find her!" Mattie's voice rose. "It's not like she wandered off in a grocery store. We're in another time!"

"I'll find her," Alex said. "Stay here. We can't stop watching for Getsky."

He jogged to the front of the barn. This time he noticed one of the double doors was open just a little. A Sophie-sized crack.

Alex slipped into the barn. Silver sprang up from his usual spot. But when the dog saw Alex, he wagged his tail.

"Sophie!" Alex whispered.

No answer. He looked at Seabiscuit's stall door. The latch was raised.

Alex's heart pounded. Suppose Getsky

had come in and horse-napped Seabiscuit!

He tiptoed to the stall and eased the door open. Peering inside, he saw Pumpkin standing with his head down, asleep. Seabiscuit lay stretched out on his side, snoring. The little dog, Pocatell, lay curled up next to Sophie.

"Sophie!" Alex said.

She lifted her head and put her finger to her lips. "Shhh. I just told Seabiscuit a bedtime story."

He walked into the stall, wading through deep straw.

"Sophie, what are you doing here? You practically gave me and Mattie a heart attack! Why aren't you guarding the door?"

"Seabiscuit was lonely," she replied.

"The horse is *not* lonely." He pointed to Pocatell and Pumpkin. "He's got plenty of friends. Come on, we have to get out of here."

Sophie frowned. "I'm not leaving my second best friend."

"What?"

"Ellsworth is my first best friend, of course," Sophie said. "But Seabiscuit is my second best friend. He wants me to stay. He likes me because I'm just like him."

"You're not like him. He's a horse!"

"I know you think I'm a human, but I'm not, really." Sophie spoke slowly, as if Alex were the five-year-old instead of her.

Alex wondered if traveling back in time had knocked something loose in his sister's head. Then he noticed how relaxed all the animals seemed. Sophie had that effect on animals. She loved all animals and they were crazy about her too. Maybe, Alex thought, animals got along with Sophie because they knew she wanted to *be* an animal.

But that didn't help their mission. They

were supposed to be on the lookout for Art Getsky.

"Let's go, Soph. If we get caught, we could get kicked off the racetrack."

"No."

Alex knew his little sister could be very stubborn. When she wanted, Sophie could make a huge scene. One of Sophie's meltdowns would be a bigger news story than the race between Seabiscuit and War Admiral.

Just then the front door creaked.

"Somebody's coming!" Alex whispered in a panic. "Quick! Hide!"

"Where?" she asked.

There wasn't anything in the stall except horses and hay. With both hands, Alex dug a hole in the deep straw. He pulled Sophie in with him and flung straw over their heads.

6

Too Many Secrets

Footsteps sounded along the floor. They stopped at the stall.

Did I latch the door behind me? he wondered. He couldn't remember.

The stall door pushed open.

Alex peered through wisps of straw. Was it Getsky?

With relief, he recognized Tom Smith. The trainer carried the homemade training bell. Mr. Smith bent down and patted the horse's neck. Seabiscuit stirred, but didn't get up.

"Hey, Biscuit," he said softly. "I'm proud of you, old boy. You're as calm as butter, the evening before the biggest race of your life."

Alex was worried that the trainer could hear his heart beating. He and Sophie were buried four feet away. Suppose Mr. Smith walked on top of them?

"You've been doing real well with this bell," Mr. Smith went on. "You're breaking fast. And you're used to the sound of it."

A piece of straw tickled Alex's nose. He twitched his nose. Any second, he would sneeze.

"Too bad the starter's bell doesn't sound like my bell," Mr. Smith said with a sigh. "I wish something would happen to the starter's bell and he'd ask to use mine. Wouldn't that be great?"

With a final pat, the trainer stood up, said

good night to the horse, and left the stall.

Alex waited until he heard the front door squeak again before poking his head out of the hay. As he helped Sophie up, he had an idea.

"Come on," Alex said to Sophie. "Mattie probably thinks we both got lost."

They slipped out the door and walked around back. Mattie jumped when she saw them.

"Where have you been?" she said. "Where were you, Sophie?"

"Long story," Alex replied. "Any sign of Getsky?"

Mattie shook her head.

"Maybe he's given up." He scanned the area. "Let's go over to the racetrack. I have to do something."

"What?" Mattie asked.

"I'll show you." Alex set off down the path.

They passed more stables and the club-house with its airy porches and cupola. Leaves rattled on tree branches and clouds scudded in the grayish-blue sky.

Outside the front gates, the kids could see the lights of Baltimore. They heard people singing, "Maryland, My Maryland." Everybody sounded happy, like they were at a party.

Alex led them past the wooden grandstands, past the electric scoreboard, and up the steps to the starter's stand. Mattie and Sophie followed.

Mattie gazed out over the main track. "What are we doing up here? The track is down there."

"I'm going to make a wish come true," he said, examining the bell built into the stand. "If Sophie can be a horse, I can be a genie."

"What are you babbling about?"

"Remember how Bobby said the horses

74

aren't using a starting gate?"

"So?" She sounded impatient.

"Since Seabiscuit and War Admiral aren't using the gate for this race, they are walking up to the starting line. When the starter rings the bell, they'll take off."

Mattie sighed. "Alex, will you please get to the point?"

"In a sec. Hold your horses."

He turned back to the starting bell. It looked like the old-fashioned alarm clock in his parents' bedroom. Alex had once pried the back off that clock to see its wires and springs.

Gripping the edge of the cover, he pulled it off and peered inside. In the fading light, he searched for two wires. Gently, he loosened the wires, and then snapped the cover back on.

Grinning at Mattie he said, "I am a genie! Your wish is my command."

"What is going on?" She punched his shoulder. "Tell me!"

"Ow! Okay, you know how Seabiscuit is trained to take off at the bell Mr. Smith made. Well, I heard him wish something would happen to the starter's bell." Alex waved his hand. "Ta-da! Wish granted."

Mattie's eyes grew round. "You fixed the bell so it won't work?"

"Yeah. Pretty cool, huh?"

"Pretty dumb! You can't do that!" She punched his shoulder again. "You can't change history, Alex!"

He rubbed his shoulder. "Quit hitting me. Don't you want Seabiscuit to win?"

"Yeah, but not by cheating!"

Sophie spoke up. "Alex isn't cheating."

"Sophie, stay out of this," Mattie told her. "Alex, fix that bell."

"It probably won't make any difference

anyway," he said. "And who's going to know? We'll just keep it a secret."

"How many times have I told you not to mess around in time, but you *never* listen!" Mattie stormed down the steps.

"Matt, wait!" Alex grabbed Sophie's hand and ran down the steps.

Mattie was halfway across the lawn, stomping toward the racetrack. Darkness had dropped, shrouding the dirt oval.

Alex and Sophie hurried to catch up with Mattie. Then Alex glimpsed movement out of the corner of his eye. Someone was walking around the track.

"Matt, get down. Somebody's out there!" Alex pushed Mattie and Sophie into a crouch.

They lifted their heads to peer into the gloom.

"Who is it?" Mattie whispered. "And what are they doing on the racetrack at night?"

A beam of light swept the ground from side to side. The figure was playing a flashlight over the track, as if looking for something.

Alex recognized the small figure. "It's the Iceman. George Woolf. I wonder what he's doing?"

The jockey stooped down and put his hand on the ground.

"Looks like he's testing the dirt," Mattie said.

"You're right!" said Alex. "If the track is too wet, the race could be called off."

As they watched, the jockey crumbled some dirt in his fingers, and then nodded as if satisfied. He stood up again and continued walking around the track, his flashlight beam swishing from side to side.

"He doesn't act like he thinks the race will be called off," Mattie said. "What do you suppose he's doing?"

Alex thought a moment. "Maybe he's found a good part of the track for Seabiscuit to run on. He doesn't want anybody to know or he wouldn't be out here in the dark."

"We won't tell," said Sophie. "We're good at keeping secrets."

"We're keeping a lot of secrets," Mattie commented. "Maybe *too* many."

"We should get back to our barn before somebody sees us," said Alex. "It's getting late." He stood up, but Mattie yanked him back down.

"What?" he asked.

"Shhh! I heard a noise in those bushes." She pointed to a nearby hedge.

Alex stared into the darkness. Gradually he made out another figure, tall with big ears. The figure crept out of the bushes, slinking away from the track.

"Getsky!" he said. "He was spying on the Iceman."

"He probably figured out what the Iceman is doing," said Mattie. "I bet he's going straight to War Admiral's team to tell them!"

"Not if we can help it. Come on!"

Alex scurried through dew-damp grass after the reporter.

"What are we going to do?" Mattie asked Alex as they skimmed across the dark lawn.

"I don't know. We'll think of something."

Suddenly someone tapped Alex's arm. He jumped and turned to look into a stern face.

A man in a guard's uniform glared at him.

"What are you kids doing out here?" he demanded. He carried a clipboard.

"Uh—just taking a walk, sir," Alex said.

"You're on private property," said the guard, "and have no business here. Tomorrow you can come in, with a ticket."

"We were just looking for—our brother!" Mattie said hastily. "He's Seabiscuit's hot walker."

"Yeah, and I'm War Admiral's mother-in-law." The guard nudged them toward the track gate. "Out you go."

He led them to the big metal gate. Swinging it wide, the guard watched until Alex, Mattie, and Sophie reluctantly trudged through it.

Then he closed it with a final clang, twisting the lock.

"What are we going to do now?" Mattie asked, after the guard had walked away. "We're locked out!"

Alex clung to the bars of the gate. "I know. And ol' Getsky is probably blabbing the Iceman's secret right this minute!"

7

On the Fast Track

Alex sank down on the ground, dejected. Mattie and Sophie knelt beside him.

Down the road, Baltimore's lights made bright yellow patches against the black sky. The entire city seemed filled with people singing the state song.

"I'm glad *they're* happy," Alex said glumly. "You know what? I think we've messed up this mission. And it's *my* fault."

"You can't help it that the guard saw us,"

said Mattie. "Maybe Getsky didn't tell anybody what he saw tonight."

"You're just trying to make me feel better," Alex said. "What good did it do to fix the starter's bell—"

Just then headlights splashed across their faces. A big truck turned into the Pimlico race-track road. The kids quickly ducked into the shadows.

The truck stopped at the gate, its engine idling. When the guard approached, the truck driver said, "Lightfoot Beverage Service. Delivery for the track kitchen!"

"You're kind of late," the guard said, flipping through the papers attached to his clipboard.

"Have you seen the traffic out there? Everybody is coming to this race," said the driver.

"Well, they can't get in till ten o'clock

tomorrow," the guard said. "Okay, you're on the list. Come on through."

Suddenly Alex realized the truck would block the guard's view for a few seconds as it drove through the gate. If they positioned themselves on the far side, they could sneak back inside!

Unlocking the gate, the guard swung it wide.

"Now's our chance!" Alex whispered. "Hurry!"

As the truck rumbled through, the kids darted in, making sure the boxy trailer of the truck stayed between them and the guard.

Alex waited until the guard closed the gates before signaling for the others to follow him. Sticking to the shadows, they crept across the lawn and past the grandstands. Soon they were back at Seabiscuit's stable.

"Might as well go to bed," Alex said. "We

can't help Seabiscuit any more tonight."

They trudged into the empty barn and threw themselves down into the hay.

This will be the first mission that we fail, Alex thought before he fell into an uneasy sleep.

The next morning, the sound of voices and hurrying feet outside woke Alex. Race day!

He sat up, poking Mattie. "Get up! You too, Soph. We've got to get to the track."

Bobby was passing their stable when they walked out. He tossed each of the kids an orange. "Here's breakfast. Come on! We're going to find out if the race is on."

Alex, Mattie, and Sophie peeled their oranges on the way to the track. Dark blue clouds quilted the sky.

"Will it rain?" Alex asked anxiously.

"I don't know," Bobby replied. "We could

use some luck on our side."

People lined the rail, but Bobby pushed through so the kids had a space up front.

A man in a gray overcoat was walking around the track.

"Who's he?" asked Alex.

"Mr. Spencer. Head of the Maryland Racing Commission," said Bobby. "He'll decide if the track is dry enough."

At last the man finished walking the entire track. He stepped up to a microphone and announced, "The track will be fast for the race by this afternoon. The race is on!"

"Yay!" Mattie and Sophie cried together.

Just then the sun came out, bathing the track in a soft glow and brightening the green grass.

Bobby grinned. "There's our luck!"

"Now what?" Alex asked Bobby.

"Now we wait until three thirty." Bobby

spotted a familiar figure. "Hey, there's George Woolf." He went over to talk to the jockey.

"Is he nervous?" Mattie asked when Bobby came back.

"The Iceman? Never!" Bobby glanced back at the track. "He wondered if the commissioner flattened the tractor tread. That's the driest part. He said he memorized the tractor path and plans to keep Seabiscuit on it."

Alex exchanged a quick glance at Mattie. Thanks to Art Getsky, War Admiral's jockey probably knew about the dry path too. What would happen if both horses tried to run on the same part of the track?

"George also told me he got a telegram from Red Pollard," Bobby went on. He laughed. "Red said Seabiscuit will win by five. Five lengths, that is."

The postcard message! Alex thought.

"I've got work to do. Look me up at post

time. I'll make sure you get good seats." Bobby dashed off toward the barns.

"What do we do until then?" Mattie asked Alex.

He shrugged. "No point watching Getsky anymore. He's already told everybody the Iceman's secret." He sidestepped a man pushing a cart piled high with boxes.

The man steered past, but the back wheels of the cart slipped off the path. The top boxes tumbled to the ground.

Alex picked one up. It was bulky, but light. "Here."

"Thanks, sonny," said the man. "That's what I get for trying to take too many boxes in one trip." Then he looked at them. "Say, you kids doing anything?"

Mattie shook her head. "Not really."

"Our parents are letting us walk around until the race," Alex added hastily. He didn't want to have another run-in with that guard.

"I'm Charlie. Would you like to help me get these hot-dog rolls to the concession stand? I've got more in the truck." Charlie jerked his thumb toward the road outside the gate. "You can have all the hot dogs and soda pop you want."

"Deal!" Alex said. He never passed up an offer of free food.

The kids carried extra boxes to a concession booth set up by the grandstands and helped Charlie unload the cart. While he returned to his truck for another shipment, Alex and Mattie stacked the boxes along the sides of the booth.

Alex admired the portable hot-dog cooker.

"I wish I had one of these in my room," he said. "I love hot dogs."

Charlie came back, his cart clinking with cases of soft drinks.

"You ought to see the mob outside!" he said. "Must be a million people waiting to get in. These bleachers only have about sixteen thousand seats. Stand back, here they come!"

The gates swung back and hundreds of people streamed through, heading for the stands.

Charlie unloaded the soft drinks and pulled his cart into the crowd. "Gotta make one more trip. If I don't come back," he yelled at the kids, "send a St. Bernard after me!"

Alex watched as row after row of the grandstands filled with people. In no time, the bleachers were crammed. Reporters jammed the press box at the top of the stands. Alex wondered if Art Getsky was up there.

People sat and stood on the porches of the clubhouse and claimed every scrap of grass on the lawn. Policemen formed a ring around the track to hold the crowd back.

When Charlie straggled to the booth again, his face was red and sweaty. "People are still coming in droves! In cars, by special trains. Everybody in the world is at this race!"

Customers lined up at the booth, clamoring for hot dogs and drinks. Charlie cooked hot dogs as fast as he could move. Mattie and Sophie set up an assembly line of mustard, ketchup, and buns on the counter.

Alex poured soft drinks into paper cups. In between, he managed to eat four hot dogs.

At last Charlie said, "You kids have been a big help, but I'm sure your parents are wondering where you are. It's almost race time. Fix yourself something to take with you."

Mattie made hot dogs for herself and

Sophie, but Alex said, "No, thanks." He was sorry he had eaten so many.

When they left the booth, Mattie asked, "Where can we sit?"

"Good question." Alex spun around.

Not one square inch of property was empty. Shoulder to shoulder, people packed the lawns and paths. They perched on rooftops and lined the fences like sparrows. They clung to telephone poles and stood on car hoods. Police were even letting people into the infield, the grassy area inside the racetrack.

The noise was incredible. Alex remembered their trip back to the 1893 Chicago World's Fair. Millions of people had attended that event, but not all at once. And the fairgoers didn't yell and scream like the people at Pimlico.

"Alex! I've been looking for you kids." Bobby dashed up, his face flushed with excitement. "It's almost time! They're heading to the saddling paddock."

They followed him through the throng toward the track. Suddenly a roar went up and thousands of people faced one direction.

War Admiral pranced down the center of the track led by Mr. Conway. He wore a white blanket and yellow ribbons in his streaming tail. His coat shimmered like silk in the sun. The horse bucked and danced. Alex thought he looked wild. And very fast.

A second roar greeted Seabiscuit. Led by Mr. Smith on Pumpkin, the chestnut horse trotted calmly to a fenced area. Seabiscuit wore a red blanket with a white **H**.

"What's the **H** stand for?" Mattie asked Bobby.

"His owner, Charles Howard. Come on." Bobby walked toward the paddock.

By the time they pushed through people,

the horses were saddled. Both trainers seemed tense and nervous. War Admiral's jockey looked stone-faced.

"Where's the Iceman?" asked Alex.

"He's playing Mr. Cool," said Bobby. "It's his trick to keep War Admiral's jockey off guard."

Just then George Woolf strolled up, dressed in white pants and a red silk jacket with the same **H** design. He swung up on Seabiscuit's back. A pretty, dark-haired woman pinned a shiny medal to Seabiscuit's saddlecloth.

"That's Mrs. Howard," Bobby said. "Look at the Iceman! He acts like he's going on a ride in the park."

Mr. Smith tightened Seabiscuit's saddle girth and adjusted the Iceman's stirrups.

At last the horses were ready.

Alex looked over at the starter's box. The men inside were scratching their heads.

Finally someone said, "The bell doesn't work. Will Mr. Smith let us use his bell?"

Alex's heart gave a flip.

"I guess." Mr. Smith didn't grin, but Alex could tell he wanted to.

Bobby ran back to the barn to fetch the bell. Then he led Alex, Sophie, and Mattie to a spot on the lawn opposite the grandstands.

The horses were led onto the track. A band played "Maryland, My Maryland," but this time no one sang along. No one spoke. The entire field was pin-drop silent. All eyes were locked on the horses.

War Admiral twirled in circles, as if he couldn't contain his need to run free. Seabiscuit plodded behind him, his head down. A lump rose in Alex's throat. Seabiscuit didn't look much like a racehorse.

When the horses stood at the starting line, the bell clanged, shattering the silence.

Seabiscuit exploded from the line at the same instant as War Admiral.

"Yes!" Alex high-fived Mattie. Mr. Smith's training with the bell had paid off!

As the horses tore around the track, the crowds leaped to their feet, cheering.

Alex leaned forward until he nearly fell over. The tension was unbearable. It was almost as if *he* were Seabiscuit, racing at top speed, spewing dirt clods with mighty hooves.

Beside him, Mattie chewed a strand of hair. "I don't think I can stand this!"

Only Sophie seemed unruffled. She smiled as she clasped Ellsworth to her chest.

"Look!" Alex cried. "Seabiscuit is ahead!"

The horses flew down the track to a deafening clamor. Crowds in the infield poured toward the rail, as if they were going to run with War Admiral and Seabiscuit.

Alex noticed the tractor tread that the

Iceman planned to keep Seabiscuit on. War Admiral's jockey shifted his horse. Now Seabiscuit's rival took over that path!

"Oh, no!" Alex moaned. Getsky must have spilled the secret, all right!

The horses peeled around the final turn, tails straight out. Then War Admiral seemed to find another gear. The sleek horse moved up alongside Seabiscuit. They ran neck and neck.

As Alex watched with a sick feeling in the pit of his stomach, War Admiral nosed ahead of Seabiscuit.

War Admiral gobbled up the track with his powerful legs. He ran like a machine. He was clearly the fastest horse.

Alex felt like crying. War Admiral, he realized, was going to win!

8

The Race of the Century

"It's over," Alex said in dismay.

"No, it's not," said Sophie, lifting her chin. "Seabiscuit will win."

"How?" Mattie asked. "He's *behind* War Admiral and they are almost around the track."

Sophie never took her eyes off the horses. "Just wait."

The crowd was going wild. Alex could feel the grandstands shaking as people jumped up and down.

The horses sliced through the air, pummeling the track with their sharp hooves. War Admiral was still a nose ahead and had almost reached the finish line.

Then Alex saw Seabiscuit's ears flatten. The brown horse stared into War Admiral's eye, as if daring him to beat him. Did the Triple Crown winner shudder, Alex wondered, or was it his imagination?

The Iceman crouched even lower over

Seabiscuit's mane and seemed to whisper in his ear. The horse surged ahead, leaving War Admiral behind!

"Woo-hoo! Woo-hoo! Woo-hoo!" Alex shrieked, springing into the air.

The fans went berserk as they broke through the line of policemen. They flooded the infield as the track announcer screamed, "Seabiscuit by three! Seabiscuit by three!"

The people at the infield rail reached out arms and hands to touch the brown horse as he sailed across the finish line. The police tried to hold back the crowds, but men, women, and children leaped over the rail and ran down the track after Seabiscuit.

The grandstands emptied like a burst dam. People gushed from the clubhouse, the telephone poles, stable roofs, and car hoods. Everyone rushed toward Seabiscuit, clapping and shouting with joy.

"Let's go!" Bobby pushed Alex, Mattie, and Sophie into the swirling mob.

They ducked under the rail and joined the wild throng racing to the winner's circle. Alex had never felt such excitement in his entire life. It was like winning the Super Bowl, the World Series, and getting all the Olympic gold medals at once!

The electric board flashed the official time—1:56 3/5.

"That's an all-time track record!" Bobby yelled. "Seabiscuit is the fastest horse to run at Pimlico—*ever*!"

The kids followed Bobby. Alex had never seen so many people in his entire life jammed into one spot. They pushed up against Seabiscuit, calling, "Georgie! Georgie!"

The Iceman looked exhausted. He had shoved his dirt-spattered goggles up on his helmet. His face was paper-white and he breathed as hard as the racehorse.

Sweat dripped from both man and horse. They had performed incredible athletic feats, Alex realized. He stared at them in awe.

Despite War Admiral's flash and speed, Seabiscuit was simply a stronger horse. Even if Getsky had told what he saw on the track the night before, it didn't make any difference.

The police struggled through and finally formed a square around Seabiscuit and the Iceman, pushing the crowds back. Then Mr. Smith rushed into the clearing. He took Seabiscuit's reins and led him into the winner's circle. Reporters and fans followed, still cheering.

"There's Getsky," said Sophie. As if he could hear her, the reporter scowled at the kids.

"I wonder if he'll get his story," Mattie said.

"Probably not the one he wanted to write,"

Alex said, but he didn't care. The *best* horse had won.

Mr. Smith was given a blanket of yellow chrysanthemums. He placed the blanket over Seabiscuit's neck. Seabiscuit turned his head, plucked out a flower, and began munching. Everyone laughed.

Then Mr. Smith pulled out a single blossom and tossed the blanket into the crowd. Another cheer went up as hundreds of hands reached for a yellow flower. In seconds, the chrysanthemum blanket was gone.

The Iceman slid off Seabiscuit's back. Charles Howard, the owner, held up the silver trophy. Reporters fired questions to the jockey, trainer, and owner.

Alex nudged Mattie. "We should go now. We've accomplished our mission."

She nodded. "It's a good time. In this mob, no one will miss us."

Alex pulled the spyglass from his pocket. He held it out to Sophie.

"No." She shook her head. "I don't want to leave. I'm staying with Seabiscuit."

"Oh, Soph, don't be silly," Alex said. "Come on." He held the spyglass closer to her.

Tears dripped down Sophie's cheeks. "I'll never see Seabiscuit again! He's my second best friend! He under*stands* me."

Alex felt a ripple of panic. Suppose they couldn't get Sophie to go home with them? What would they tell their parents? *Sorry, but we left Sophie back in* 1938.

Alex bent down so he was level with Sophie's eyes. "Soph," he said. "If you come home, I promise I'll play horses any time you want. Every single day. Twice a day, even."

Sophie's bottom lip trembled. "Really?"

"Me too," Mattie put in.

"All right. Good-bye, Seabiscuit," Sophie

said sadly. "I'll miss you!" Then she grasped the middle of the spyglass.

Alex sighed. "Hurry," he told Mattie.

Mattie held the other end.

Alex felt relieved when the spyglass tingled beneath his fingers. The strange designs rose on the brass tube. He closed his eyes.

Red and white sparkles—Seabiscuit's racing colors—flickered behind his eyelids.

Then—*whoomp*!

He landed on the familiar floor of the tower room. When he opened his eyes, he saw Mattie and Sophie standing next to him.

"Another mission down," he said, putting the spyglass back into the desk.

Mattie headed toward the bookcase-panel. "Stay here. I'll be right back." Then she vanished through the panel.

Alex noticed Sophie staring out one of the long narrow windows as she clutched

Ellsworth. He shivered, thinking how close they had come to not bringing Sophie back

Suppose it happened again? And he and Mattie couldn't convince her to return? He decided to start being a better big brother right away.

"Hey, Soph," Alex said. "At least you picked a winner. You had faith in Seabiscuit when I didn't."

She rubbed one eye. "I'll always miss him."

The bookcase-panel swiveled as Mattie crawled through again. She carried a big book.

"I thought I remembered this," she said, flipping it open on the floor. "It's all about horses."

Sophie wandered over, interested. "Look! There's Seabiscuit!"

"We know Seabiscuit won the race," Alex said. "What are you looking for?"

"The story about the race between Sea-biscuit and War Admiral. Here it is!"

Mattie tilted the book so she could read it. "It says here that on the day of the race, the starter's bell mysteriously didn't work—" She flicked a glance at Alex. "And that they borrowed Tom Smith's homemade redwood bell to use in the race."

"I told you it would be okay!" he said, grinning. "I didn't mess with history after all."

"I'm not so sure," Mattie said, closing the book. "But at least you didn't change history."

"Seabiscuit was meant to win the race because he was the fastest, strongest horse," Alex said. "Get the letter and let's go downstairs. I'm hungry."

Mattie retrieved the envelope from the desk. "How about a hot dog?"

"Ugh!" Alex made a face. "I don't ever want to eat another hot dog in my life!"

Mattie led the way through the bookcase-panel. Alex got down on his hands and knees to follow her.

He looked back. Sophie stood by the desk, easing open a small drawer.

"Soph? You coming?"

"Yes."

Before he turned, Alex thought he saw a flash of something small and yellow disappear into the drawer. And then he smelled the crisp, autumn smell of chrysanthemums.

Dear Mattie, Alex, and Sophie:

I hope you three enjoyed your trip back to your old home state, Maryland. And Alex, you finally got to play on a team again! But you also learned that sports stars aren't always quarterbacks. Racehorses—and jockeys—share amazing athletic abilities.

Men have depended on horses for centuries. Horses carried knights into the Crusades and other wars. But horses were also raced. England's Queen Elizabeth I raised racehorses.

Turkish and Arabian horses were faster and stronger than English horses. Three horses—the Byerley Turk, the Darley Arabian, and the Godolphin Arabian—were bred with English horses, beginning in the early 1700s, to produce a Thoroughbred. Today all Thoroughbreds are descended from those three stallions.

American colonists loved horse racing. In 1665, a pasture in Long Island became the first racetrack. The first American Thoroughbred, Bulle Rock, was brought to Virginia in 1730.

Horse racing became less popular in the early part of the twentieth century. In 1929, the value of stocks declined and banks closed. By 1933, millions of Americans were out of work. They stood in "breadlines" for free food. Although a new president, Franklin Roosevelt, developed programs to help people find jobs, the Great Depression lasted from 1929 to 1939.

During this time, Americans needed hope. They found it in a mud-colored racehorse with crooked front legs. His name was Seabiscuit.

Seabiscuit was born in 1934, descended from Man O'War. War Admiral, son of Man O'War, was actually Seabiscuit's uncle! Seabiscuit preferred sleeping and eating to racing. He lost his first seventeen races. But after Charles Howard bought the horse, Tom Smith became Seabiscuit's new trainer. Smith understood Seabiscuit. He knew the stallion wasn't lazy at all. With Red Pollard as Seabiscuit's jockey, the horse began winning races.

Besides silver trophies, cash prizes are awarded in horse races. The Santa Anita "Hundred Grander" alone gave the winner $100,000. Year after year, Seabiscuit lost that race.

George Woolf, the Iceman, rode Seabiscuit to victory in the Pimlico match race, making the little horse an American hero. At the time of the match race between Seabiscuit and War Admiral, Red Pollard was in the hospital. His leg had been smashed in a riding accident. Doctors said he would never walk again, much less ride.

In 1939, Seabiscuit tore a tendon in his left front leg. His racing days seemed to be over too. But horse and jockey did not give up. Red worked with Seabiscuit until they both grew stronger. When they ran the "Hundred Grander" in 1940, Seabiscuit and Pollard left all the other horses and riders behind.

Everyone loved Seabiscuit. They stood along railroad tracks to see his train car.

They bought Seabiscuit wallets and hats. They played Seabiscuit board games. The little horse that gave people hope during troubled times died on March 17, 1947, at age fourteen.

For your next trip, Time Spies, dress warmly!

Yours in time,
"Ms. Hawley"

TIME SPIES MISSION NO. 7
MAKE A SPY LIGHT

Most of the time, spies don't want to be seen. But there will be times when you need to see where you are going! Or you will need to find something in the dark, like the Iceman did. A flashlight will come in handy.

In the 1890s Conrad Hubert, founder of the Ever—Ready battery company, invented the first flashlight. Hubert fashioned the "electric hand torch" with a battery, a paper tube, and a lightbulb. Because the light of his torch flashed briefly, the name "flashlight" stuck.

You can make your own flashlight with items from around your house.

WHAT YOU NEED:

Aluminum foil

Small lightbulb from an old flashlight

Toilet-paper tube

Electrical tape

2 D-cell batteries

Scissors

WHAT YOU DO:

1. Tear off a piece of aluminum foil 7-1/2 by 4 inches.
2. Fold it lengthwise into a strip 1/2 inch wide.
3. Tape the two batteries together, end to end. Make sure the positive end (+) of one battery touches the negative end (-) of the other battery.
4. Cut the toilet-paper tube from top to bottom. Cut twelve slits at one end, 1/2 inch apart.
5. Place the batteries in the paper tube. Tape it so that the batteries fit snugly inside the tube. Make sure the positive end of the battery sticks out about 3/4 inch.
6. Fold the bottom slits of the paper tube, leaving a hole for the negative end of the battery. Tape.

7. Tape the foil strip to the side of the tube, leaving 3/4 inch on both ends.
8. Tape the bulb to battery at the top. Make sure the end of the lightbulb touches the positive end of the battery.
9. Touch one end of the aluminum foil to the negative contact at the bottom. Touch the other end to the side of the bulb. Light!

How do you trick a troll?

Do vampires sleep?

Why worry about yuan-ti?

All the answers (and more!)
can be found in

A PRACTICAL GUIDE TO MONSTERS

Written by famed wizard Zendric, this fully illustrated
guide is chock full of fascinating monster facts! Discover
intimate details about the habits and habitats of each
magical beast, pore over maps of their lairs, and find out
the best tools and tricks to overcome them.

FOR AGES SIX AND UP

Join the Knights as they battle monsters, solve mysteries and save their town from certain destruction.

COLLECT THEM ALL!